SWI

ROTHERHAM LIBRARIES AND NEIGHBOURHOOD HUBS

30/5/23		
1 5 JUN 2023		

This book must be returned by the date specified at the time of issue as
the DUE DATE FOR RETURN
The loan may be extended (personally, by post, telephone or online) for
a further period, if the book is not required by another reader, by quoting
the barcode / author / title.

Enquiries: 01709 336774

www.rotherham.gov.uk/libraries

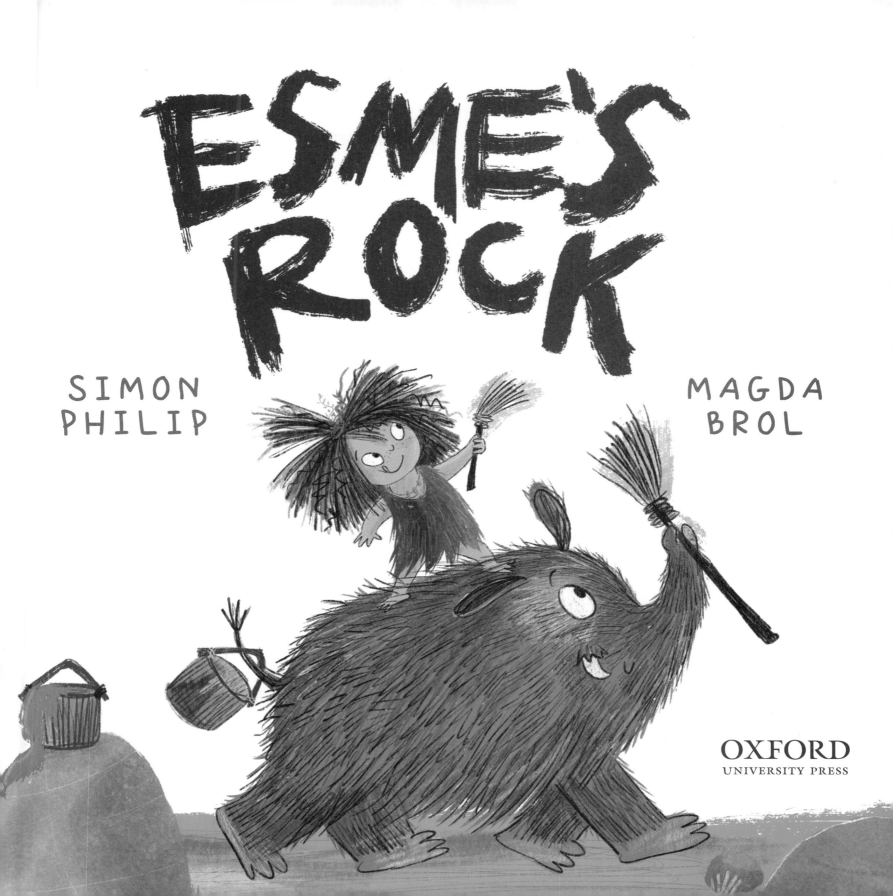

ESME'S ROCK

SIMON PHILIP

MAGDA BROL

OXFORD
UNIVERSITY PRESS

Once upon a very, **Very** long time ago, when the Internet was hopeless, a young girl woke at the crack of dawn.

Esme was very small—so made mammoths
look even more **mammoth** . . .

. . . very **energetic**

. . . very **curious**

. . . and very **friendly**.

She also had a VERY loud voice.

'HELLO!'

It was great for
keeping **big** things with
sharp teeth away . . .

But not for keeping birthday surprises secret.

'Doris will **love** her party!'
said Esme.

'Yippee! **A party!**'
Doris immediately whooped.

Whispering wasn't easy, but Esme was determined **not** to spoil
her best friend Morris's upcoming surprise.

On Morris's birthday, Esme's voice was a VERY effective alarm clock—whether or not everyone wanted it to be.

'Happy birthday, Morris!'

Luckily, for once, an early start was exactly what was required.

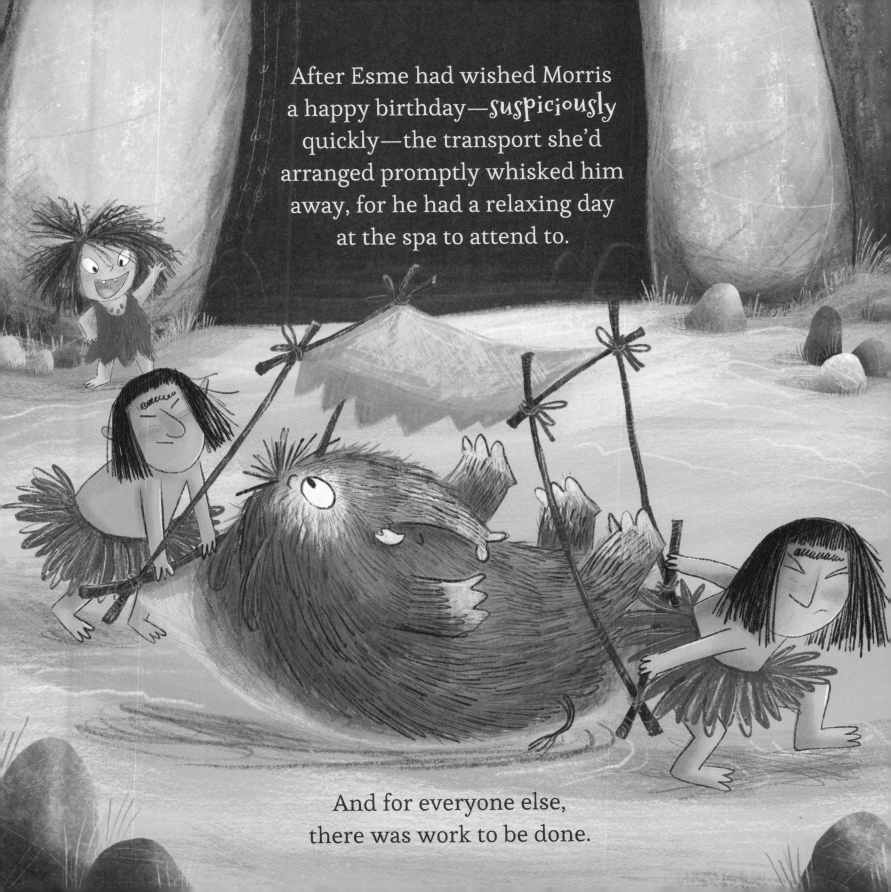

After Esme had wished Morris
a happy birthday—suspiciously
quickly—the transport she'd
arranged promptly whisked him
away, for he had a relaxing day
at the spa to attend to.

And for everyone else,
there was work to be done.

But when they realised how much work
Esme's surprise involved, they gasped . . .

'You want us to paint
that whole rock?
In a day?'

'Yes,' Esme said,
untroubled, 'so we'd
better crack on.'

Soon, everyone—and **everything**—was up to their neck in paint . . .

. . . whereas Morris, blissfully relaxed and unaware of the surprise in store, was up to his neck in mud.

By lunchtime, the painters were exhausted, but when they stepped back to admire their progress . . .

. . . they realised they'd barely made any.

'H-A—is that all we've done?'

HA

Esme was exasperated.

'It's not funny!' she said, her voice rising into a shout.

'Too loud, Esme!' the others warned.

But she couldn't contain herself.

'We need more painters or Morris's birthday surprise will be ruined!'

Esme's voice echoed across valleys . . .

and villages . . .

. . . and into curious ears.

It was heard by **everyone**.

Well, **almost** everyone.

Back at the rock, the mood was as blue as the paint on the stone. Everyone could only hope that Morris somehow hadn't heard Esme's outburst.

And with **SO** much rock still left to paint, they thought about giving up.

But, just as everyone was about to pack up their brushes and paints, they received a shock of their own . . .

. . . when the strangers arrived—
and unpacked *theirs*.

Suddenly, the wall
seemed **much** smaller.

HAP

And, with everyone working together, they didn't stay strangers for long.

As for the rock, thanks to Esme's particularly clear instructions, it was soon finished— which left just one more thing to do . . .

Morris **hurtled**
home at once . . .

His surprise at the
surprise *surprised* everyone...

HAPPY
BIRTHDAY!
SURPRISE!
MORRIS

...and the celebrations
rocked!

And, whilst Esme
promised she'd practise
her quiet voice, everyone
saw there was a time
and a place for her
unique volume, too.

The **time** was whenever word needed to be sent
or people brought together, and the **place** . . .

... was **Esme's Rock.**

OXFORD
UNIVERSITY PRESS

Great Clarendon Street, Oxford OX2 6DP
Oxford University Press is a department of the University of Oxford.
It furthers the University's objective of excellence in research, scholarship,
and education by publishing worldwide. Oxford is a registered trade mark of
Oxford University Press in the UK and in certain other countries

First published 2021

British Library Cataloguing in Publication Data

Data available
ISBN: 978-0-19-277502-3

1 3 5 7 9 10 8 6 4 2

Printed in China

Paper used in the production of this book is a natural,
recyclable product made from wood grown in sustainable forests.
The manufacturing process conforms to the environmental
regulations of the country of origin.